For Kai Santiago Lacera. We love you forever, no matter what you eat.
Thank you to our parents, Dick, Monia, Doris, and Jorge. We love you!
—M.L. and J.L.

Text copyright © 2019 by Megan Lacera and Jorge Lacera
Illustrations copyright © 2019 by Jorge Lacera
Children's Book Press, an imprint of LEE & LOW BOOKS Inc.,
95 Madison Avenue, New York, NY 10016
leeandlow.com
Edited by Jessica V. Echeverria
Designed by Ashley Halsey
Production by The Kids at Our House
The text is set in P22Stanyan
The illustrations are rendered digitally
Printed on paper from responsible sources
Manufactured in China by Jade Productions
10 9 8 7 6 5 4
First Edition
Library of Congress Cataloging-in-Publication Data
Names: Lacera, Megan, author. | Lacera, Jorge, author, illustrator.
Title: Zombies don't eat veggies / by Megan Lacera & Jorge Lacera;
illustrated by Jorge Lacera.
Other titles: Zombies do not eat veggies
Description: New York: Children's Book Press, an imprint of
Lee & Low Books Inc., [2019] | Summary: Although Mo's parents insist he eat
zombie cuisine, Mo craves vegetables and strives to get them to taste recipes
made from his hidden garden. Includes recipes.
Identifiers: LCCN 2018028760 | ISBN 9781620147948 (hardcover: alk. paper)
Subjects: | CYAC: Zombies—Fiction. | Vegetarianism—Fiction. |
Family life—Fiction. | Secrets—Fiction.
Classification: LCC PZ7.1.L17 Zom 2019 | DDC [E]—dc23
LC record available at https://lccn.loc.gov/2018028760

ZOMBIES
DON'T EAT VEGGIES!

by Megan Lacera & Jorge Lacera
illustrated by Jorge Lacera

Children's Book Press,
an imprint of Lee & Low Books Inc. • New York

Mo was a zombie with a deep, dark craving.
It was dreadful. Devious. Absolutely despicable.

Mo loved to eat vegetables.

He grew all kinds of veggies in his hidden garden.

And then in his secret kitchen, he crafted celery, tomatoes,

and carrots into *delicioso* meals that he devoured with delight.

Mo's mom and dad did not love vegetables. Not. One. Bit.

Veggies were yucky! Disgusting! *¡Que asco!*

They were not allowed at the Romero's dinner table.

READY TO CHASE SOME HUMANS IN THE MARATHON NEXT WEEK, *MIJO?*

ENDURANCE TRAINING FOR ZOMBIES

Zombies were supposed to eat zombie cuisine like brain cakes, brain stew, and brain-and-bean tortillas.

Mo's parents insisted that their *niño* eat only zombie food.

Mo tried to convince his mom and dad to give peas a chance.
He sneaked in vegetables whenever he could.

But Mo's attempts were fruitless.
His parents wanted him to accept
who he was—a zombie.
And zombies don't eat veggies.

Mo knew he did not like zombie cuisine.
And he couldn't imagine letting go of spinach
or cucumbers or kale forever.

If zombies are only supposed to eat zombie cuisine,
Mo started to wonder if maybe he wasn't a zombie after all.

Day after day, Mo wondered how he could make his parents understand his love of veggies.

His tomatoes were tantalizing.

His cucumbers crispy.

The peppers, perfection.

Add onions, some garlic,

a touch of cilantro, and . . .

GAZPACHO!

Holy aioli!
Mo had an idea.
His best one yet.

Mo grabbed his book of recipes.
His fingers flew across the pages . . .

. . . until he found it. The recipe for a tomato-and-veggie-filled soup.
He was sure the tomatoes would make it look bloody and gloopy,
just like a zombie dish. His parents were going to devour it!

Mo chopped and diced,

blended and pureed,

perfected and poured.

Finally, the soup was finished.

Mo carefully shuffled it over to the house for dinner . . .

KEEP OUT!

Peligro

DANGER!

!

SARAH
BELLUM

TRY SOME ARM-PANADAS, *MI AMOR*. PRIME CUTS! *MIRA*, I MADE SPICY MAN-NAISE.
DORI-TOES (FOR DIPPING)
ARM-PANADAS

They dug in.

Mo closed his eyes and sucked in his breath.

This was it.

They'd savor the soup.

They'd ask for *mas*.

Mo imagined breakfasts, lunches, dinners, snacks.
All VEGETABLES!
Raw, cooked, steamed, and fried.
Forever and ever.
He saw all his dreams coming true.
Until . . .

Mo's parents did not like the soup.
Not. One. Bit.

¡DIOS MIO! THIS SOUP TASTES LIKE . . . LIKE . . . VEGETABLES! YUCK!

Mo's heart sank to his toes.
His plan was a bust.

MAYBE OTHER ZOMBIES DON'T EAT VEGETABLES, BUT I DO. MOM AND DAD, I'M DIFFERENT.

BUT I'M STILL ME. MAURICIO ROMERO. YOUR *NIÑO*. YOUR MO.

Mo reminded his parents that he liked chasing humans as they ran in marathons.

And he promised he'd always cheer for Dad during championship brain-eating competitions.

He also loved doing the zombie shuffle under the moonlight with Mom.

He was a zombie. A Romero. He just liked to eat vegetables.

Mo's parents loved their son and finally accepted
that it was okay to be different.
They even promised Mo they would eat more veggies—for him.

FRIED
FIDDLEHEAD
FERNS

ARTICHOKE
HEARTS AND ELBOW
MACARONI

PATA-CONES

The Romeros knew that most zombies don't eat veggies.
But they were more than zombies.
They were a family.

MO'S GARDEN GAZPACHO
(AKA BLOOD BILE BISQUE)

Make sure an adult is available to help!

Serves four

INGREDIENTS

5 vine-ripened tomatoes, chopped,
   or 1 16-oz. can chopped tomatoes
1 red pepper, seeded and roughly chopped
1 small onion, roughly chopped
½ cucumber, roughly chopped
2 cloves garlic
10 basil leaves
1 tbsp. olive oil
Handful chopped cilantro (to garnish)

DIRECTIONS

1. Put the tomatoes, pepper, onion, cucumber, garlic, and basil into a food processor or blender. Blend until smooth.
2. Add in the olive oil and mix until just combined.
3. Pour into bowls.
4. Top with cilantro, to taste.
5. Serve cold for traditional style. Hot is yummy too!
6. To add even more fun, take balls of mozzarella and stick a raisin in the middle of each. Place two mozzarella balls in each bowl of soup to look like eyes!

Zombie Finger Foods

Make sure an adult is available to help!

INGREDIENTS

celery sticks
peanut butter (Nut allergy? Sunflower butter works too.)
blanched almonds or sunflower seeds still in the shell
strawberry jelly or jam

DIRECTIONS

1. Fill celery sticks with peanut butter or sunflower butter.
2. Dip the widest end of an almond or sunflower seed in the jelly and stick the other end into the peanut butter or sunflower butter at the end of a celery stick.
3. Serve on a plate and swirl some of the jelly "blood" around it.
4. Do the zombie shuffle to celebrate your yummy creations!

THE ROMERO FAMILY'S FAMOUS SHOCKAMOLE

Make sure an adult is available to help!

INGREDIENTS

2–3 small avocados
½ small vine-ripened tomato, chopped
2 cloves garlic, finely chopped
juice from a fresh lime
1 tbsp. chopped red onion
sea salt
plantain chips, carrot sticks, or cucumber wedges

DIRECTIONS

1. Cut the avocados in half. Discard pit seeds. Scoop the avocado flesh into a large bowl.
2. Do the monster mash! Mash up those avocados.
3. Add the garlic, lime juice, tomato, and red onion. Mash it up!
4. Add sea salt to taste and mix.
5. Serve with plantain chips, carrot sticks, or cucumber wedges. Everything tastes delish with shockamole!